To
Sam
with love
from
your cousins
Kate Paddy
& Ciara

hug x

A PARRAGON BOOK

PUBLISHED BY PARRAGON BOOK SERVICE LTD.
UNITS 13-17, AVONBRIDGE TRADING ESTATE, ATLANTIC ROAD,
AVONMOUTH, BRISTOL BS11 9QD

PRODUCED BY THE TEMPLAR COMPANY PLC,
PIPPBROOK MILL, LONDON ROAD, DORKING, SURREY RH4 1JE

COPYRIGHT © 1996 PARRAGON BOOK SERVICE LIMITED

ILLUSTRATED BY STEPHEN HOLMES

DESIGNED BY MARK KINGSLEY-MONKS

PRINTED AND BOUND IN SPAIN

ISBN 0-75252-035-0

CHILDREN'S STORYTIME TREASURY

Tales of Brer Rabbit

P

|| · PARRAGON · ||

Many years ago on a cotton plantation down in the deep south of North America there lived an old black slave called Uncle Remus. Every evening he would sit in his creaky old rocking chair on the shady verandah and tell his tales to anyone who would care to listen. With eyes as round as saucers, the little children gathered around his feet and when Uncle Remus was quite comfortable he would begin.

He told about the days long, long ago when animals would stroll around town arm in arm, talking and laughing just the same as us folks. Some of the animals were good little animals, and some of them were bad. And some of them were so full of mischief there was no telling just what they might do next. Just the same as us folks, you could say!

These are just a few of those stories that Uncle Remus first told all those years ago.

Brer Rabbit and the Bramble Patch

Brer Fox was up to no good. He had found some black tar and turpentine and had made himself the strangest little doll you ever saw.

"This here's my Tar Baby," he said as he sat her in the road. "She's going to wait for Brer Rabbit!"

Brer Fox hid in the bushes and soon he could hear Brer Rabbit coming along the road.

"Mornin'!" says Brer Rabbit, tipping his hat politely to the Tar Baby. But she says nothing, and Brer Fox lies low. "And how are you this fine mornin'?" asks Brer Rabbit. But the Tar Baby still says nothing.

"If you don't say howdy to me I'm gonna bust your nose!" shouted Brer Rabbit, and blip! he smacked the Tar Baby on the side of her head. Well, that was a big mistake for now his hand was stuck. He smacked the Tar Baby again. Second big mistake!

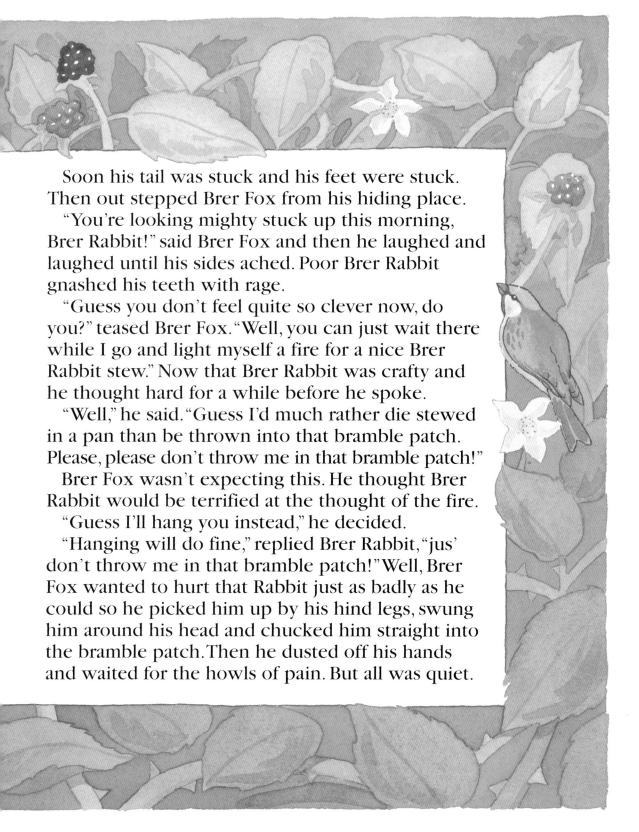

Soon his tail was stuck and his feet were stuck. Then out stepped Brer Fox from his hiding place.

"You're looking mighty stuck up this morning, Brer Rabbit!" said Brer Fox and then he laughed and laughed until his sides ached. Poor Brer Rabbit gnashed his teeth with rage.

"Guess you don't feel quite so clever now, do you?" teased Brer Fox. "Well, you can just wait there while I go and light myself a fire for a nice Brer Rabbit stew." Now that Brer Rabbit was crafty and he thought hard for a while before he spoke.

"Well," he said. "Guess I'd much rather die stewed in a pan than be thrown into that bramble patch. Please, please don't throw me in that bramble patch!"

Brer Fox wasn't expecting this. He thought Brer Rabbit would be terrified at the thought of the fire.

"Guess I'll hang you instead," he decided.

"Hanging will do fine," replied Brer Rabbit, "jus' don't throw me in that bramble patch!" Well, Brer Fox wanted to hurt that Rabbit just as badly as he could so he picked him up by his hind legs, swung him around his head and chucked him straight into the bramble patch. Then he dusted off his hands and waited for the howls of pain. But all was quiet.

After a while he heard Brer Rabbit's voice calling out to him quite cheerfully from the top of the hill.

"Why, thanks Brer Fox," he cried. "Thanks for setting me free from that Tar Baby. And thanks for dropping me off in that old bramble patch. Why, that's one of my very favourite places, you know! I was born and raised in that bramble patch!"

BRER RABBIT AND THE WELL

Brer Rabbit was hard at work in the garden
with Brer Fox, Brer Raccoon and Brer Bear.
The sun was hot and he was fed up.

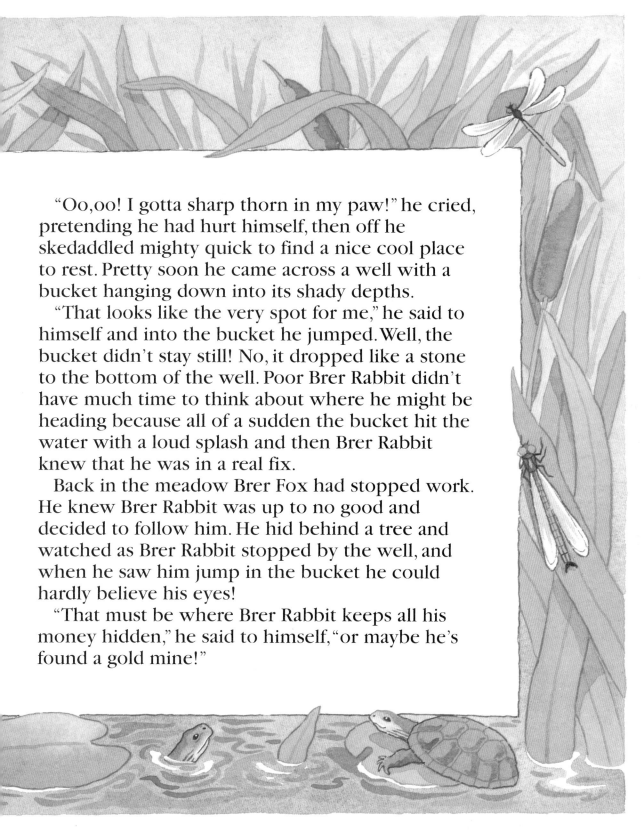

"Oo,oo! I gotta sharp thorn in my paw!" he cried, pretending he had hurt himself, then off he skedaddled mighty quick to find a nice cool place to rest. Pretty soon he came across a well with a bucket hanging down into its shady depths.

"That looks like the very spot for me," he said to himself and into the bucket he jumped. Well, the bucket didn't stay still! No, it dropped like a stone to the bottom of the well. Poor Brer Rabbit didn't have much time to think about where he might be heading because all of a sudden the bucket hit the water with a loud splash and then Brer Rabbit knew that he was in a real fix.

Back in the meadow Brer Fox had stopped work. He knew Brer Rabbit was up to no good and decided to follow him. He hid behind a tree and watched as Brer Rabbit stopped by the well, and when he saw him jump in the bucket he could hardly believe his eyes!

"That must be where Brer Rabbit keeps all his money hidden," he said to himself, "or maybe he's found a gold mine!"

Slowly he crept to the well and peered over the edge. There wasn't a sound to be heard. Down at the bottom of the well poor Brer Rabbit sat hunched up in his bucket, hardly daring to twitch a whisker. Suddenly a loud voice echoed down the well.

"Howdy, Brer Rabbit," called Brer Fox. "What are you doing down there?" Brer Rabbit thought hard.

"I'm fishing," he replied. "There are some mighty fine fish down here, Brer Fox. Why don't you come and get some for yourself?"

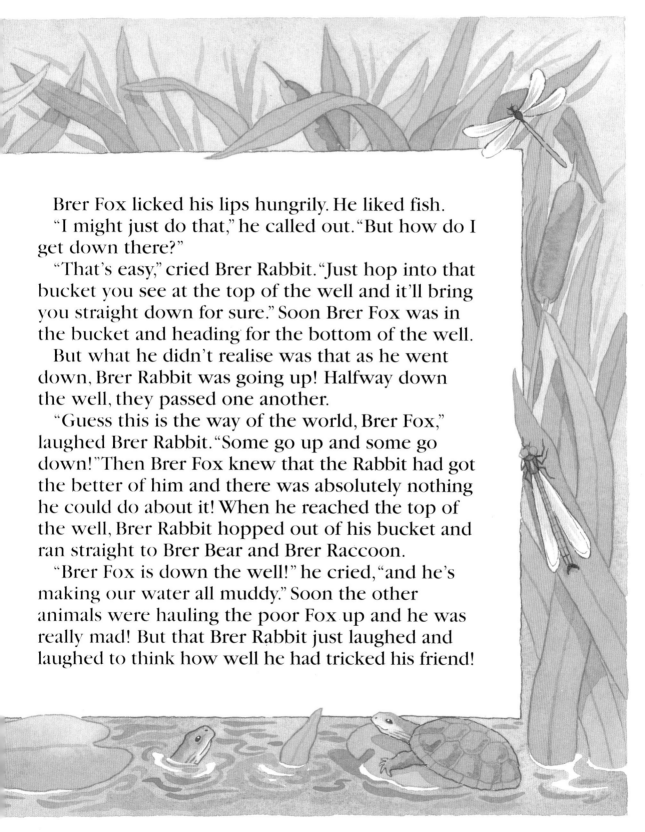

Brer Fox licked his lips hungrily. He liked fish.

"I might just do that," he called out. "But how do I get down there?"

"That's easy," cried Brer Rabbit. "Just hop into that bucket you see at the top of the well and it'll bring you straight down for sure." Soon Brer Fox was in the bucket and heading for the bottom of the well.

But what he didn't realise was that as he went down, Brer Rabbit was going up! Halfway down the well, they passed one another.

"Guess this is the way of the world, Brer Fox," laughed Brer Rabbit. "Some go up and some go down!" Then Brer Fox knew that the Rabbit had got the better of him and there was absolutely nothing he could do about it! When he reached the top of the well, Brer Rabbit hopped out of his bucket and ran straight to Brer Bear and Brer Raccoon.

"Brer Fox is down the well!" he cried, "and he's making our water all muddy." Soon the other animals were hauling the poor Fox up and he was really mad! But that Brer Rabbit just laughed and laughed to think how well he had tricked his friend!

BRER RABBIT AND THE PEANUT PATCH

Brer Fox was mighty proud of his peanut patch. He weeded it and watered it and looked forward very much to the day when he could eat a fine crop of nuts. But Brer Rabbit had his eye on that self same peanut patch and one morning, when the peanuts had grown big and ripe, he crept through the fence and helped himself just as sassy as you please.

When Brer Fox saw that somebody had been scrabbling in and out of his plants he grew mighty mad.

"I'm going to make a trap and catch that no-good varmint who's stealing my peanuts if it's the last thing I do," he said to himself. Soon he had made a fine trap with some rope and a slim hickory sapling and he positioned it right next to the hole in the fence.

The very next day Brer Rabbit came sashaying down the road towards the peanut patch. He wriggled all unsuspecting through the hole in the fence and what a fright he got when he suddenly found himself whisked up in the air and dangling by his back paws on the end of a rope! There he swung, to and fro, while he tried his best to think of a way to free himself.

Just then Brer Bear came ambling down the road. "Howdy, Brer Bear!" called Brer Rabbit.

"What in tarnation are you doin' up there?" asked the astonished Bear as he spotted Brer Rabbit above him.

"Why, I'm earning a dollar a minute guarding the peanut patch for Brer Fox," replied the wily Rabbit. "But I reckon I've earned enough money now," he added. "Do you want to take over from me?"

Brer Bear looked at him doubtfully. "Do you reckon I could do it?" he said. Brer Rabbit nodded encouragingly.

"Why, it's easy as pie," he said. "I'll show you what to do!"

Soon Brer Rabbit was standing on the ground and Brer Bear was swinging in the air.

"Brer Fox, come out!" shouted the naughty Rabbit. "Here's the rascal who's been stealing your peanuts!" Out shot Brer Fox with a stout stick in his hand.

"So that's your game, is it?" he cried, and he set about poor Brer Bear with his stick. The Bear tried in vain to explain that he was guarding his peanut patch for him but the furious Brer Fox did not believe a single word of it.

And where was Brer Rabbit? Why, he was long gone. Long gone!

BRER RABBIT AND THE RIDING HORSE

B rer Rabbit and Brer Fox were at it again. No matter what one of them did, the other had to try and do it just a little bit better.

One day Brer Rabbit was taking tea with his good friend, Miss Meadows. "I feel sorry for that pesky Brer Fox," he confided. "When I see the poor thing struggling to keep up with me it makes me want to weep. He's just not in my league." He shook his head pityingly. "Foxes have always been inferior to Rabbits. Why, my daddy used to use Brer Fox as his riding horse many years ago."

Miss Meadows looked most astonished to hear this news and when Brer Fox next came to call she asked him if it was indeed true that he used to be Brer Rabbit's father's riding horse. Brer Fox grew red with rage and it took some time before he could talk.

"Miss Meadows," he said at last. "I am gonna make that Brer Rabbit eat those words and spit them out!"

Soon Brer Fox was hammering upon Brer Rabbit's front door. Brer Rabbit wanted him to go away so he called out of the window.

"I am glad you are here, Brer Fox!" he said. "Please run and fetch me the doctor for I am ill."

"Well, isn't that a shame," replied Brer Fox, "because Miss Meadows and the girls are having a party and they would dearly love you to come." Then Brer Rabbit thought for a while.

"I am not well enough to walk," he said. "You will have to carry me upon your back." Brer Fox didn't like this idea at all but he finally gave in.

"I will need a saddle and a bridle," added Brer Rabbit. "I shouldn't want to fall off before I get there." Soon Brer Fox was fully kitted up with saddle and bridle and Brer Rabbit sat squarely on his back looking for all the world like a regular race jockey. And then he had some fun! He dug in his heels and that poor Brer Fox had no choice but to gallop off down the road.

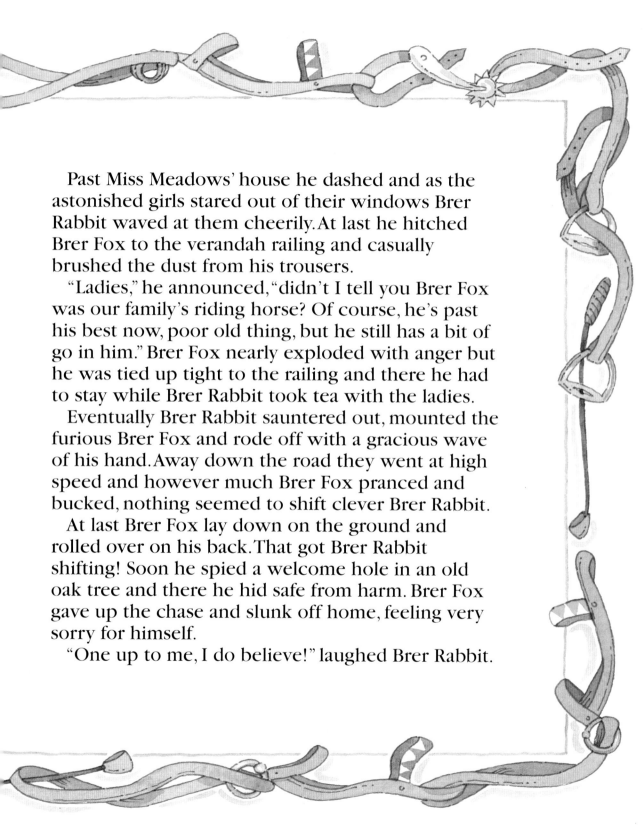

Past Miss Meadows' house he dashed and as the astonished girls stared out of their windows Brer Rabbit waved at them cheerily. At last he hitched Brer Fox to the verandah railing and casually brushed the dust from his trousers.

"Ladies," he announced, "didn't I tell you Brer Fox was our family's riding horse? Of course, he's past his best now, poor old thing, but he still has a bit of go in him." Brer Fox nearly exploded with anger but he was tied up tight to the railing and there he had to stay while Brer Rabbit took tea with the ladies.

Eventually Brer Rabbit sauntered out, mounted the furious Brer Fox and rode off with a gracious wave of his hand. Away down the road they went at high speed and however much Brer Fox pranced and bucked, nothing seemed to shift clever Brer Rabbit.

At last Brer Fox lay down on the ground and rolled over on his back. That got Brer Rabbit shifting! Soon he spied a welcome hole in an old oak tree and there he hid safe from harm. Brer Fox gave up the chase and slunk off home, feeling very sorry for himself.

"One up to me, I do believe!" laughed Brer Rabbit.

BRER RABBIT'S GOOD CHILDREN

Brer Fox was hungry. His tummy was a-rumbling and a-grumbling and he knew the only way to quieten it was to find some food.

"I wonder if Brer Rabbit has any tasty titbits hidden away inside his house?" Brer Fox wondered and he peeked inside the window. There he saw Brer Rabbit's children frisking about their hole without a care in the world. The hungry Fox licked his lips.

He knew that the little rabbits were all alone because he had just seen Brer Rabbit and Mrs Rabbit inspecting Brer Turtle's cabbage patch. He tapped on the glass with his paw.

"Let me in," called Brer Fox in a wheedling voice, "and I'll just sit and wait for your ole daddy to come home." Now these little rabbits knew Brer Fox and they were polite little rabbits, so they opened the door and pretty soon Brer Fox was sitting comfortably and watching them with a strange look in his eye.

Presently he pointed at a large piece of sugar cane leaning up against the wall.

"I sure am hungry," he said. "Break me off a piece of that cane, will you?" Now Brer Fox knew there isn't anything much tougher in the world than sugar cane and he hoped the rabbits would fail, for then he would have an excuse to eat them. The little bunnies pushed and pulled at the cane but it wouldn't even bend. Just then they heard a bird on the roof singing to them.

"Use your toofies and gnaw it and then it will break."

So the rabbits set to with their sharp teeth and soon they laid a sweet, juicy piece of cane at Brer Fox's feet.

Brer Fox thought again. He would have to find them something harder to do. Then he saw a sieve on the wall.

"I'm mighty thirsty, rabbits!" said he. "Take that sieve and fetch me some water from the spring." The rabbits ran down and dipped the sieve in the water, but to their dismay the water just trickled straight out again. Then they heard the little bird singing once again.

"Line it with clay, then the water will stay."

The rabbits did as they were told and soon they had carried a sieve full of water back to Brer Fox. He was furious to see that this plan had also failed.

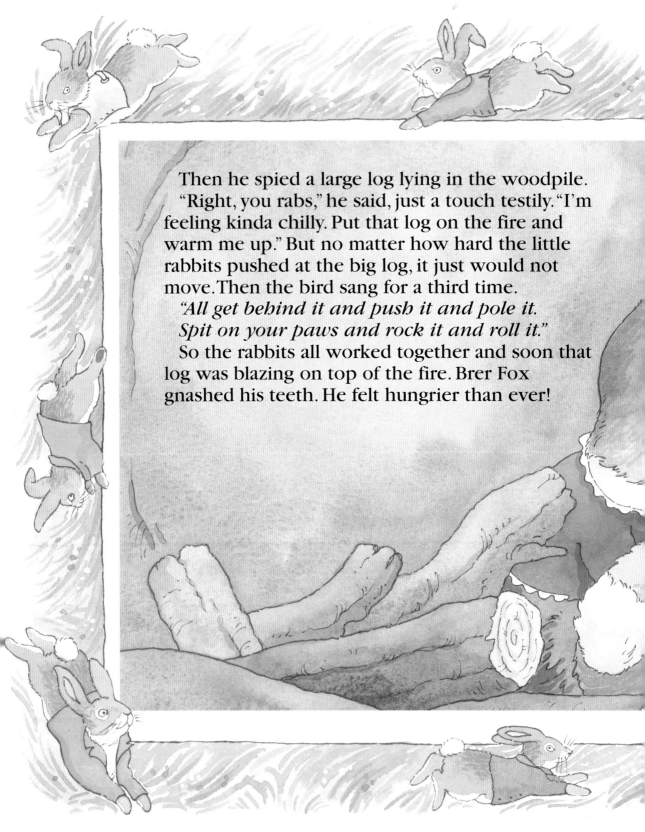

Then he spied a large log lying in the woodpile.

"Right, you rabs," he said, just a touch testily. "I'm feeling kinda chilly. Put that log on the fire and warm me up." But no matter how hard the little rabbits pushed at the big log, it just would not move. Then the bird sang for a third time.

"All get behind it and push it and pole it.
Spit on your paws and rock it and roll it."

So the rabbits all worked together and soon that log was blazing on top of the fire. Brer Fox gnashed his teeth. He felt hungrier than ever!

Just then who should walk in but Brer Rabbit himself and my, how his little children were pleased to see him. He took just one look at Brer Fox and knew straightaway what he was up to.

"Do stay and have tea with us, Brer Fox," offered Brer Rabbit. "You look mighty peckish." But something in Brer Rabbit's voice made Brer Fox want to get out of the house as quickly as possible and with a sheepish grin he made his excuses and left.

How Miss Cow was Milked

Brer Rabbit was thirsty. He watched Miss Cow grazing peacefully in the meadow. He would love a drink of milk, but how was he to get it? "Howdy, Sis Cow," he said after a while.

"Could you do me a little favour, Sis Cow?" Brer Rabbit went on, all big eyes and innocence. Miss Cow stopped chewing and looked up at him.

"I would dearly love to eat some of those persimmons," explained Brer Rabbit, pointing to a large tree growing in the meadow. "If you shake the trunk, then they will fall down off the branches and we can share them."

Now Miss Cow was a friendly creature and all too happy to oblige. She ran at that tree full tilt, but what a shock she had when her horn got stuck in the trunk!

Off ran that wily Brer Rabbit and pretty soon he was back with all his little children and each one carried a clanking milk pail! The children clustered so tight around Miss Cow that you could hardly see her and right in the very centre of them sat Brer Rabbit on a three legged stool, milking away for all he was worth.

He filled pail after pail with the sweet warm milk and when he was done he tipped his hat politely.

"I realised you might be stuck there all night and figured that you'd be pretty sore carrying all that milk, so I thought I'd help you out. Kind of a good deed, you might say," and with that he set off for home.

Miss Cow was furious! With one mighty moo, she pawed at the ground and pulled her horn free. Why, she was so mad that Brer Rabbit could have sworn he saw real steam coming from her nostrils!

She raced down the meadow after him and the earth trembled under her hooves. But at the bottom of the field was a large bramble patch and that lucky Rabbit was soon safe inside the bushes. How he laughed.

"There isn't one animal I know who can get the better of ole Brer Rabbit!" he boasted happily.

Fishing for the Moon

One day Brer Rabbit decided to play a trick on his friends, Brer Fox, Brer Wolf and Brer Bear. "I'll invite them to meet us down at the millpond tomorrow evening and we'll go fishing," he told Brer Turtle. The next night the animals set off with their nets and rods and maggots.

But when they got to the pond Brer Rabbit gasped in amazement, then shook his head.

"I reckon they'll be no fishing for us tonight," he said, "for the moon has fallen in the water."

Sure enough, there she lay quivering in the pond and the animals all tut-tutted and scratched their heads.

"Only way we'll get some fishing done tonight is if we drag her out," said Brer Rabbit at last.

"Good idea!" agreed Brer Turtle and soon Brer Fox, Brer Bear and Brer Wolf were in the pond with a net.

"You've nearly got her!" cried Brer Rabbit as he tried hard not to laugh.

"We just can't seem to catch her!" wailed Brer
Fox. Deeper and deeper they went until suddenly
they were out of their depth and thrashing the
water so much it was a wonder they didn't empty
the pond! At last they scrambled onto the bank,
quite miserable.

"Better luck next time!" said Brer Rabbit grinning
broadly and he winked at Brer Turtle. Why, it was
almost *too* easy to trick those silly animals!

OTHER TITLES IN THIS SERIES INCLUDE:

AESOP'S FABLES

GRIMM'S FAIRYTALES

HANS ANDERSEN'S FAIRYTALES

JUST-SO STORIES

NURSERY TALES

TALES FROM THE ARABIAN NIGHTS

WIND IN THE WILLOWS